this book belongs to

_____

Once upon a time, there lived a great warrior. His name was Prince Rama. Prince Rama was married to Princess Sita. She was beautiful inside and out.

Deep in the dark jungle lived a terrible Rakshasa named Ravana. He was the evil demon king of Lanka. What a frightful sight he was. With ten heads and twenty arms, he was the most fearsome creature in the land.

The horrid king had heard how kind, beautiful and good Princess Sita was, and he wanted her for himself. He devised a cunning plan to make her his wife.

Ravana sent his servant Maricha disguised as a beautiful golden deer.

He knew that Sita would not be able to resist such an enchanting animal.

As predicted, Sita instantly fell in love when she set eyes on the deer.

She wasted no time in telling her husband Rama about the deer.

"Rama, nothing would make me happier than to have such a beautiful animal as my pet," Sita told him.

Rama knew it would be difficult to catch the deer, but he replied, "For you, my dearest princess, I would do anything."

Rama asked his little brother Lakshman to help him catch the golden deer. Lakshman agreed, and before leaving, he drew a circle on the ground around Sita.

"Do not leave this circle, Sita," he warned. "If you stay inside the lines, you will stay safe."

Ravana's master plan had worked. Without Rama in the way, he was able to get to Sita without any interruption.

Ravana disguised himself as an old beggar and went to visit Sita. "Please help me, I am hungry and have not eaten or drunk for days," he pleaded.

Sita was very kind. She went inside to fetch some food
and water for the poor man. As she handed the man the
food, she stepped out of the circle that Lakshman had
drawn.

The beggar suddenly turned back into Ravana. He grabbed Sita, pulled her onto his mighty flying chariot and flew back to Lanka, his island.

Sita dropped her jewelry to the ground, hoping it would leave a trail for Rama to follow.

Prince Rama returned home, disappointed because he could not get Sita the deer. The brothers agreed it must have been some kind of trick, and unfortunately they were right.

"LOOK! Sita has been kidnapped!" shouted Lakshman.

Rama and his brother saw one of Sita's necklaces, then another, and they followed the trail of jewels through the forest until...

they came across the monkey God, Hanuman.

Hanuman had many super powers. He could run faster than the wind and fly like a bird. He could even shrink to the size of a tiny ant or, in the blink of an eye, grow taller than the mountains.

"Could you please help me find my wife?" Rama asked.
"Of course I will help you. I know you are a good man,
and I will do my very best," said Hanuman. Rama gave
him his ring to give to Sita.

Hanuman searched for many days and nights. He traveled through forests and up mountains.

He leapt across the ocean to get to the island of Lanka.
He was brave and determined to find the princess.

Eventually, he found Sita. She was locked up inside
Ravana's prison.

Hanuman handed her Rama's ring. Sita held on tight and waited in anticipation. She knew it wouldn't be long until Rama would come for her.

The loyal Hanuman took the news of his discovery back to Rama.

They gathered a huge monkey army to help them rescue Sita.

"We can't all fly and leap like you, Hanuman. How will we get across the ocean?" asked Rama.

"We will use stones and build a giant bridge," replied Hanuman.

Once the bridge was finished, the monkey army rushed across to find Ravana and his army.

The battle began and lasted for ten whole days.

It was one of the mightiest battles the world has ever seen.

Near the end of the ten days, Rama and Hanuman's army started to get tired. Ravana and his evil army would not give up.

Suddenly, Rama spotted the perfect opportunity to use his magic arrow that the Gods had given him. He shot Ravana down with the magic arrow.

The evil demon King Ravana fell.

He had been defeated.

Rama and his love, Sita, were finally reunited.

They started their long journey home on that very night.

It was a new moon, which was perfect for new beginnings and fresh starts. But this also meant it was very dark.

All the people throughout the kingdom lit diyas and left them in their windows and doorways to help guide Rama and Sita back home.

That night, there were more diyas than stars in the sky. It felt like the whole world was illuminated, not only with lamps but with goodness, power and good luck.

They followed the trail of lights all the way back home.

Everyone celebrated their safe return.

And still to this day, the celebrations continue every year. We call it Diwali, the festival of light. At Diwali, we remember the great story of Rama and Sita.

We light lamps and set off fireworks to remind ourselves and each other that light triumphs over dark and good triumphs over evil.

For more information:
hello@littlebookwallah.com

Second paperback edition September 2020

ISBN 978-1-80098-002-0